WINDCHIMES: LIFE AND DEATH

WINDCHIMES: LIFE AND DEATH

Dyes Funeral Service

AMY L. DEANES

Superior Publishing LLC.

CONTENTS

This book is dedicated to my
Wayne, Treasure, Atiya, Atori, Uzziah, Treasure, Jr., Tru

Thanking God for doing it again.

CHAPTER 1

In the Beginning

Walking through her extended hallway, looking in every mirror as she passed through, patting her face with a facial sponge, Nori was almost late to the next funeral. Her head was all over the place! How could he, her ex, possibly want half of her business and she inherited this before she even knew him.
As she let her garage door down backing out into the driveway, she remembered her phone...

"Dang it!" She hit the steering wheel as if it was its fault that she had forgotten, but the steering wheel yelled out a loud, " hooooonnk!!!!"
She got out to run back inside and as she grabbed her phone from the counter, it begin to ring. It was Wilson, her facial expression changed from frustration to HEAVEN-LATION.

He was her new limo driver. I'll tell you how he looks later, but with a name like WIL-SON...OKKKK YOU FEEL ME.

"AYYY!! Nori answered showing every teeth in her head.

" Boss lady," he smiled at himself in the mirror of that white stretched limo truck.

"Where you at Sunshine?"

"Sunshine catching hell right now, I'm on my way"... she backed that Range Rover out of the driveway like it was on fire.

"I got you boss, take your time, you know Imma handle it." Wilson smiled.

"AT THE FUNERAL"

Sooo of course Nori was too late to ride in the funeral procession, so she parked her wine colored Range Rover across the street from the Civic Center. One last booger and eye matter check before getting out. As her black heels hit the pavement it seemed like the world was set in motion. She walked with class, head held high as if she never met a problem in her life, but she was battling on every side and the world didn't know.

As she entered the building, the family came slowly behind. The organ played but it could not drown out the murmuring and commotion at the casket. She immediately sped up to see flashes from phones and her employees trying to control the flow of people. As she made it closer, she could clearly see that her new makeup and hair artist had done a masterpiece on the wrong body. Nori could not let it show on her face, but why in the world would Cymphonee put lashes on Mrs. Judy B? And not the small lashes, but the lashes that looked like two ceiling fans and Lord what was this diamond on her chin? And who in the world told her to put baby hair around her edges? And whyyyyyyyy in the world was she wearing hot pink lipstick and a shiny pink prom dress?

Nori begin to sweat, there was absolutely no coming back from this. Cymphonee dressed Mrs. Judy B with the wrong orders.
And then Mrs. Judy B had a smile. Lord what a disgrace! Wilson all the way from the back noticed that something was wrong with Nori, he made his way to her as if he was in a Calgon commercial swimming through the waters trying to get to her...

"What's goooooing?" He couldn't finish the sentence, he saw it with his own eyes,

"Mrs. Judy B! Got DANG Cymphonee MONKED this up!" I got it!! I got it!!" Wilson always had it.

"What can you do at this point?," Nori was standing there in a panic while the staff held the family back. But Wilson ran out of the side door and set fire alarm off. Wilson ran back in yelling,

"Everyone out now!"
Of course hearing the fire alarm, the people picked up the pace going in the other direction. He then, signaled the Pastor to ask everyone to leave the building immediately to go back to their vehicles. Wilson realized they couldn't take the body without being seen. He kept calling Cymphonee's phone but there was no answer. Wilson was thinking now.

"Running out of time! Dang Cymphonee!! I know! I know!" Wilson was talking to himself.

"What you got under that dress Sunshine?" Nori looked puzzled, "There is no time for...wait are you serious??""

"Yes gimme that dress you got on!" Wilson had his game face on.

"Wilson, no!" Nori was looking flushed.

"Our image is on the line here Boss lady!" Wilson was serious, " Either we change your dresses out or let the State Senator's family and colleagues see what a circus we made with his wife, the lovely and classy Mrs. Judy B Morgan." Wilson pulled those ceiling fan lashes off Mrs. Judy B. He wiped that hot pink lipstick off and he went to work! He started ripping that prom dress off, rhinestones were flying everywhere like pop-corn popping in the skillet. All of Dyes Funeral Service workers were in disbelief.

"While y'all looking, everyone needs to be working! Nori go on in the back and send that dress back up here! Here, take my suit coat and go on home and get re-dressed, I got it until you get back and give me your lipstick.'
She had no problem with that things were looking up again, she reached into her purse and pulled out her makeup bag,

"Here!" she started pulling off her suit coat and Doris one of her employees unzipped it in the back.

"Thank God I wore a full slip today!" She handed off her black suit to Mrs. Judy B, the Senator's Dear wife.

"I just need a hat now to go on her head," Wilson battled with Mrs. Judy B's large arms trying to get that body in that dress.

"Tell Pastor Cook, I need his wife hat ASAP!" I'll give it back after service." Wilson and the Pastor had history together they were homeboys from another city.
Doris walked as fast as she could, clucking to the side door exit where the Pastor and wife were parked. Without any hesitation she came back holding it in the air like she had won a trophy.

Wilson put that hat on Mrs. Judy B head, pow-
dered her face and pulled that diamond off her
chin. He put a long stemmed rose on her chest
and she was perfect.

THE MELT DOWN

"She looks better today than she did in high
school!" Sonny Boy said grinning, He was another
employee of Dyes Funeral Services. And he was a
force to be reckoned with.
"I remember she didn't want to give me the time
of day!" He walked up to the casket with a stank
look on his face.
"NOW LOOK AT-CHA JUDY with the Booty! I
REMEMBER WHEN YOU SAID Ova yo dead body!
Look at ya nigh Judy!!! I'M ova yo dead body!!!"
Ya looking like a cheap clown nigh! JUDY YOU
AIN'T NO!"
"Sonny Boy what the hell has gotten into
you?" Wilson interrupted his ranting and raging.
"This woman dead, she don't know what you
talking about! Chill out Maine, GOT DANG!"
Wilson was upset now no time to waste with
foolery.
"I bet she know!" Sonny Boy hit the casket,
and made it rock..
" Hey heeey!!!!!" Wilson pushed Sonny Boy in the
chest "Chill out now Maine! GOT DANG NOW!
Let this woman rest in peace nigh she already
been through it"
"Forget her! Forget her! You just tryna impress
Nori Hell! Nori ain't want you, you broker than
me!!" You driving her cars, trucks, and stretched
out limos and what nots! This ain't yo funeral
home son!" Sonny Boy was hissing and growling
he was in rare form.

Wilson was about to grab Sonny Boy but Doris hopped in the middle.

"Come on Sonny you been drinking again!" Doris tried to escort Sonny Boy to the back but he faked her out and turned around and ran towards Wilson, but he slipped on a rhinestone and hit the floor sliding like a bowling ball and knocked over Mrs. Judy B plants.

Doris and Eldredge grabs him. Wilson just shakes his head. The Fire Marshall comes in and confirms that everything was ok. That they could restart the funeral. Sonny Boy then cried out like a baby...

"Judy B! I would've did anything, anything, anything, just tell me Judy B!"

The side door opens and the Pastor comes back in grinning.

"Wilson, you still good ole boy!" You always knew what to do! Y'all ready to kick it back off? Let's send Mrs. Judy B off with a blast homeboy!!"

Pastor Cook and Wilson fist bumps. Wilson smiled showing those pretty white teeth and deep dimples,

"Let's do it!"

CHAPTER 2

Graveside Service at Banyon

Charles, the hearse driver opened Mrs. Judy B's casket one last time and Wilson pulled Pastor Cook's wife lavish black hat from her head. Poor Mrs. Judy B didn't have this much excitement when she was living.

The hearse led the way to the Goodfellow Burial site. All four white Cadillac trucks, one behind the other taking Mrs. Judy B away beautifully.

"A WINDCHIME"

As Nori pulled off behind the last truck, she could only remember the sermon, not that Mrs. Judy B was looking a hot mess, not that Sonny Boy had a melt down, not that Wilson set the fire alarm off to borrow time to perform a miracle, but she remembered what Pastor Cook said,

"The Time is Now! For there is a season for all things. What will you do in your season? Will you be stagnant or will you flow like a river? Pastor Cook said, The Windchimes that hang by a string are not just hanging there being beautiful but they also work, they sway to and fro all day long and they make the most beautiful, heavenly harmonic sound, all with the help of God's wind. That's how we get to and fro because of God's wind in our bodies, we are not just put here to be beautiful but we are here to glorify our Creator. If you can't think of anything else, think of the Windchimes. Momma Judy was definitely a Wind-chime."

As they arrived at the cemetery, Nori watched Wilson hand the Pastor his wife's hat. Mrs. Judy B Morgan another success!

BANYON CREEK

"Lord what a hot day for a graveside service." Wilson thought to himself as he pulled up with the Hott family in the back of his limo. "Somebody gonna pass out today!"

He opened the door and five of the Hott's got out purple t-shirts and jeans and a few skirts flooded the area. R.I.P. DUFF-DUFF with a picture of a lights skinned young man with long hair posing in front of a building. As the Pastor was getting ready to call the service to order there was a loud outburst of cursing. The crowd immediately turned their attention to that direction. There it was...

Grandma Hott and Auntee Red were digging and rolling down their skirt and jeans, fire ants had invaded them. Another lady ran trying to aid grandma, while trying to help grandma get out of her loafers, they slipped down. But grandma was slapping and patting her legs, waddling trying to get back up with that skirt half way down.

"Hammercy Hammercy!" Things were getting more and more intense and out of control.

Grandma light blue bloomers were out for the world to see, she was shaking it fast and dropping it low... it looked like they were doing an African dance, especially when Paw Paw Hott noticed his wife's BEHIND was out. That was a no-no! He was limping to her so fast, he had almost forgot that he had a cane.

"Emma Jean, wait now your tail out, Yo tail is out Emma!" He seemed to not understand that her body had been invaded by ants. Grandma just kept on, chanting,

"Hammercy Lord, Hammercy!" Paw Paw Hott grabs her from behind to be a covering, but the look didn't go down so well, it totally looked like the Hot Boyz, Back that Thang Up video. He was trying to cover and she was trying to rub the stings of the ants off. A horn started to blow and Oh my macaroni and cheese Oddie Lee, Jr. had driven across the cemetery, he was coming to get his momma. It was a hot day and the HOTTS put on a show....Oddie Lee yelled,

"Come on momma and Red! Git in!" Papaw was walking so close behind grandma you would have thought they were con-joined twins.

"Put that camera down, don't film dis!" Papaw Hott was yelling at the people mostly his own family, but yet holding on to Grandma Emma Jean. What a sight for the blind to see!

LAUGHTER IS GOOD FOR THE SOUL
Wilson had laughed so hard he walked off and ran into the rest of the Dyes crew hiding and laughing. There were tears but not sorrowful tears, the laughing gas had been spilled in that hot cemetery.
The Pastor had the hardest time trying to regain their attention after this....

"Laughter is good for the soul, it's like medicine. Proverbs 17:22 tells us, "A merry heart doeth good like a medicine: but a broken spirit drieth the bones.
Romans 12:15 says Rejoice with those who rejoice, weep with those who weep. But look at the Lord, He uses everything He created. Who would have thought that the ants could bring so much laughter to a Home Going service. Use everything that the Lord has given you. Don't die with your gifts and talents never being used. Don't die and never have unwrapped the gift that God has given you. I know as we think about Lil Duff and how young he was, he left not one gift unopened. At a young age, he lived a full life. He cared for others, made people laugh, he fed the hungry, gave clothes to those in need. This young man encouraged me to get the building next to the church to feed the homeless, and a place to get hot showers and snacks. At his age, he had LOVE in his heart. He was a prankster, yes, he did things yes, but we are all human beings, and we all have faults. But that's why Jesus died, because the Good Lord knew that we would have faults. As we get ready to commit this young man back to the earth...Always remember to use your gift to help others.
We will always remember Duff, he always knew how to make people laugh, he could even make you laugh at yourself. I'd be the first to say that Duff-Duff, Bro Anqwon had something to do with this. He always kept Momma Emma Jean on her toes, Duff you outdone yourself today brother!" Everyone had calm down. Dyes Funeral Service had regained their positions. Nori smiled at Wilson and gave the nod of approval.

Anqwon Gist aka DUFF-DUFF another successful service.

Nori sent the text message out,

"Mandatory meeting tomorrow at 3:30 ALL EM-PLOYEES MUST BE PRESENT!"

CHAPTER 3

The Body Call

Everyone drug into the meeting...because really no one likes a meeting. The long wooden table was shining like it was wet.... well maybe because it was wet....
Everyone started coming in around 3:20. Cymphonee was already there doing make-up. Willie was already there bringing in supplies. Doris came in carrying a plate of food. Charles came in limping a little, said his gout had flared up again. The new guy, a youngster, DisVon eased in with his shades on and a black and mild behind his ears. The receptionist, Lee Lee, came down the hallway humming, Wilson came in looking like Mike Vick, and Nori Dyes, the Owner and Operator sat at the head of the long table smiling at Dyes Funeral Service Family.

"Well, we will give SonnyBoy and Big John a few more minutes they may be riding together. But I can go ahead and say that we have been having some great success lately. And we have had some epic fails, but we've got to give it up for Wilson with the SAVE on Mrs JudyB.

"Yeah, I apologize that was all on me," Cymph-pnee looked with a humble spirit.

"I was trying to make sure I followed every-thing to the T, but it was the wrong body." She dropped her head,

"Baby hold your head up" Mrs. Doris said eating her cabbages, corn, pork steak and corn bread,   "We've all made mistakes baby! Ain't no-body perfect in here or out there, it's just a "When-thing" when it's gonna happen."

"That's right Cymphonee! I applaud you for your awesome work! You had old DUFF-DUFF glowing girl and Mr. Pete looked like he was just sleep. You're Amazing Cymphonee that's why I hired you...I saw your work and your heart honey."
The door busted open and SonnyBoy came in dragging like he had a rough morning and Big John came behind hm with his arm in a sling.

"Evening everyone!" SonnyBoy sat at the table and Big John went to the other side and sat down.

"Hey yall!" Big John smiling.

"What the hell is this is on this table wet?!" SonnyBoy slinging his arms and the water went into Doris cabbages and on to Big John's lip.

"Dang Sonny! You slung that mess on my lips, what is it?!"
Doris was about to eat her greens and Willie went in for the dive, he knocked Doris's fork across the table and yelled,

"Embalming fluid!" Everyone stood up,

"Embalming fluid??!!" Doris flipped her plate over like it was all she could do to keep from eating. Big John shot out running like he had just come out of a canyon,

"My Mouth! My mouth burning!" Wilson and Nori ran after him to the bathroom. Doris looked at Willie,
"How in this big old world did embalming fluid get in my BLAMING greens Willie Earl?!! Doris fists were balled up like she wanted to fight, "and then on Big John mouf!"

"I wasted it on the tttttable, I thought I gggggot it all up!" Willie stuttering to get his words out.
The phone started ringing it was a body pick up call.

"DisVon you and Charles got a call. Charles, this will be DisVon's first body pick up, do you need SonnyBoy to go with yall? Lee-Lee looking at the notepad, "789 Logan Street
67-year-old black male, survived by his wife, and his children still on scene and the police will stay on scene until we get there. Seems like there has been a disturbance."

"Logan? My folks live over there, what was the name Lee-Lee?" SonnyBoy walked closer to hear.

"67 years old" SonnyBoy cut Lee-Lee off.

"Lord I hope it ain't Jerry Mane! 67 it's got to be Jerry! Yall come on!"

"Wait SonnyBoy you might not need to go if it's family!"
SonnyBoy walked on out as if he didn't hear Lee-Lee. He started beating the walls and hollering,

"Jerry Mane! Two sista chilluns!! Two sista chilluns mane!"
Doris was still standing and fuming,

"I just want to know why Embalming fluid got in my humping greens!" Willie was pointing to the table, the top wasn't closed good and I knocked it over and I went and got," he pointed down the hall and SonnyBoy come back in hollering,

"Jerry Mane gone! %$# ! =/÷$." SonnyBoy was so dramatic.

" Mr. Sonny don't you go, Willie will go with Charles and DisVon." Lee-Lee stood there holding the notepad.

"I'm going, this personal, this personal, this is personal now Lee-Lee!"

"Willie, Willie you better leave, with them done messed up my humping food!" Doris was bit her bottom lip trying not to say anything else.

CHAPTER 4

The Body Call
Continues...

Willie ran to get some more stuff to clean the embalming fluid off the table. Doris was so upset her temper was jumping like she was chewing gum. DisVon was in disbelief at everything going on.

"Yall riding with me come on now, My cousin gone mane!" SonnyBoy was in rare form.

"Noooo SonnyBoy you can't drive sir, it's obvious you're inebriated." Lee-Lee lil wavy pony-tail was bouncing up and down and she was taking long strides to get to SonnyBoy. "You need to sit this one out OK?"
SonnyBoy wasn't hearing it,

"I've been here since this here gul folks open this place, and you wanna give me awdas (orders) and still wet behind the ears."

"SonnyBoy sit down! Cause-of you my dinner is gone, up slinging embalming fluid on my plate! You need to go wash your arm off! Every time I look around you melting down and crying, you need to get some help!" Doris was looking for a fight. SonnyBoy turned like he was on the matrix.

"Who ask you Doris? Who ask you a got!" Big John walked in.

"Aaayyy SonnyBoy noooo man don't do that come on, let's go to the call... come on DisVon!" SonnyBoy looked at Doris like she was stinking! He pointed his finger at her.....

"Watch yoself wit me, aint nonna Clarence! Let's ride John John." He walked out with DisVon, Big John and Charles loafing slowly behind. Dyes Funeral Services rings again. It's another body pick up call. Lee-Lee goes outside to let them know there's another call, so Wilson and DisVon go one way and John, Charles and SonnyBoy go to Logan.

'We will go over to the Nursing home on Stone Rd and get that body and come check on yall on Logan. Wilson was talking to John John as he was going to the other truck...John was in the passenger seat, Willie was driving and SonnyBoy was sitting in the back.
As they pulled off Nori, Lee-Lee and Cymphonee stood in the parking lot shaking their heads.

"SonnyBoy needs to get some help his drinking is getting out of hand." Lee-Lee suggested thinking about his behavior lately.
They were a street over from Logan and SonnyBoy had messed around and rubbed his eyes,

"Ahhhhhhhhhhhhhhhhh sh&%!" Charles was looking back in the rear view trying to see what was happening. Big John looks back,

"What's wrong SonnyBoy?" You might not need to go on this call, I'll call Wilson to come get you!"

SonnyBoy was still hollering and cursing,
    "$#/^#! @@$/%%!%%%$PULL OVER MY ##$&^*< EYES!!!! THEY BURNING LIKE A REAL HELL!" SONNYBOY HAD RUBBED THAT EMBALMING FLUID IN HIS EYES.
    "MANE YEEN WASH YOUR HANDS?!!" BEFORE BIG JOHN COULD FINISH, SONNYBOY WAS ROLLING IN SOMEONE'S YARD.
    "PUT IT IN PARK CHARLES DANG MAN, THIS MAN DONE JUMPED OUT THIS" BIG JOHN HAD GOT OUT WITH HIS ARM IN THE SLING. CHARLES WAS SLOWLY COMING AROUND THE SIDE. It appeared as if Big John was fighting with Sonny but the homeowners had no idea what was going on. Charles was reaching out to the home-owner with both hands out with a plea for help. This black lady wearing a red bonnet, red paja-mas with duster on top looked amazed at what was going on.
    "We need some milk! Go get some milk!" Big John had found a water hose and he was skeeting SonnyBoy in the face.
    "I'm burning like the bush in the Bible days!!!" SonnyBoy was saying everything that came to mind. Charles was still trying to convince the homeowner to go get some milk. But the police pulled up....no questions were asked.
    "Hey everyone down!" Police got out yelling and holding his taser.
    "Nooo" Charles was holding his hand out trying to explain, but the Cop wasn't hearing him.
    "Get down now!!" SonnyBoy was still hollering and John was washing him down as he fought with the burning in his face.

   "Mr. Officer, he needs some milk!" Charles talked as slow as he walked. The officer aimed the taser at Big John,
"Get down now!" The officer was serious.
"He's got embalming fluid in his eyes Mr. Officer!" Big John tried to explain.
"He needs some milk" Charles was still trying to get milk, but nothing was going right. By this time Jerry Mayne came through and saw SonnyBoy, his first cousin on the ground... and immediately Jerry Mayne ran into Big John. ..

CHAPTER 5

The Body Call Still Going

(dedicated to Frances Deanes, Momma)
Jerry Mayne could only see that Big John was drowning his cousin on the ground and he was fighting to get away, when in actuality he was only trying to help him get embalming fluid out of his eyes. Nevertheless Jerry Mayne jumped in and took Big John to the ground. The police was in disbelief, he didn't know who to tase, it was just too much going on ... but Charles was getting closer to him so the officer tased Charles, because Charles was slowly coming to him with his hands out trying to explain. Charles let out the loudest groan like a black bull in heat...Charles groan could be heard for at least 2 blocks, he locked up and hit the pavement. Jerry Mayne was trying to get his cousin SonnyBoy up off the wet grass and Big John was like a turtle on its back.

"First Cuz I got em! I got em 2 sista chilluns right here like back on the block!" SonnyBoy couldn't see Jerry Mayne but he heard his voice...

"JerryMayne!!! That you cuz?? I thought you were dead cuz! I can't see Mayne got embalming fluid in my eyes.... wait you jumped on Big John? Go help him up Jerry Mayne, he was tryna get the stuff out my eyes man!" Jerry Mayne led his first cousin back to their ambulance. And then Wilson pulled up.

"Hey what's going on?" He saw Charles on the ground screaming in slow motion, he saw Big John on his back, he saw the supposedly-dead-guy leading SonnyBoy to the ambulance. Wilson was unsure of the scene. He looked at the new guy,

"DisVon you take the body on to the building, you don't need to be involved in whatever this is." He opened the passenger door, because he was allowing Disvon to get used to driving on pick up calls. DisVon looked a little nervous.

"Ahhhhh Wilson, do I get her out by myself?" Well Willie at the building he will help you." Wilson hit the hood of the car and walked into chaos. DisVon drove off going about 3mph. Wilson ran to get Big John up and led him to the truck. He then walked over to the Police to see what was really going on. The officer could not explain, because he didn't understand what was going on himself. Charles groans sounded like a woman in labor. Wilson pleaded for the Officer to let Charles up and try to explain what was what. They got Charles up, Jerry Mayne had got SonnyBoy back in the back seat. And apologized to Big John. Wilson now puzzled about Jerry Mayne resurrection. So he walks back to the truck and ask SonnyBoy,

"How did your cousin come back to life?" Wilson was puzzled. SonnyBoy tries to explain everything.

MEANWHILE

DisVon is now driving about 80 mph the lady in the back had passed gas. It was long sounded like someone dragging a chair across the floor. It was loud and loose. DisVon heart was moving faster than the vehicle. His nerves had gotten so bad, his leg were trembling uncontrollably. Tears had welled up in his eyes... he was trying to call his Momma but his hand was trembling so bad, he dropped the phone in the floor board. He pushed his rear view mirror up, he was going to Make sure that he didn't see anything. He pulled up to the light. His body was trembling so terribly that he was unable to control his face, or his hands and legs. DisVon was so scared until he was out of control... he glanced at the car next to him and noticed that they were staring at the back of his car

They begin to point at the back of his car. DisVon heart sank....he didn't want to, but he pulled the rear view mirror back down.... and Have Mercy.... the body bag was sitting up straight. The lady in the back had risen. DisVon opened the door to run, but instead he peed as his legs gave away with him and he hit the highway, DisVon's body gave away to the gravity underneath him. He passed out in the middle of traffic...

CHAPTER 6

The Six...More Chaos

More Chaos

"When everyone gets back we will try to finish up this meeting.... we've got a graveside and a church funeral tomorrow. I want everyone on their p'sand q's
speaking of the meeting, everyone has sure been gone for a while," Nori looked at the time.

"Gal ain't no telling bout SonnyBoy nem" Doris had calmed down and cleaned up the area where she flipped her plate. Feet came clucking down the long hallway. Lee-Lee was running,

"Mrs. Doris!! Mrs. Doris! Mr. Clarence on his way down here to fight SonnyBoy!" Lee-Lee was out of breath...

"Fight SonnyBoy!" Doris and Nori jumped up at the same time.

"Noon-Noooo, Doris call Clarence we've got a Wake in another hour, we don't have time for this drama!" Nori was rubbing her head on both sides.

"This bougie chick has already struck my last nerve about this wake today....I can't deal with anything else right now." Nori was feeling like she was about to experience a major breakdown and anything else extra in her life right now was going to do her in. Doris left out with her flip phone switching like there was a fire. Lee-Lee and Cymphonee sat with Nori, no words, just silent stares, it wasn't good. Nori was under so much stress, no one had the words to pull her out. (it's dangerous to be in the midst of people that don't know how to pull you out of the pit). The phone rang and as Lee-Lee answered it was DisVon.

" Mane somebody need to come git this body mane... look ain't gone be able." DisVon sounded like he was crying or whining or he had a toothache or something. Lee-Lee kept her composure and walked out of the conference room.

"DisVon what you mean? Yall didn't get the body?" Lee-Lee trying to understand what was going on

"The body here at the Four-Way mane sitting in this traffic. Ainnnn gone just leave know what I mean, I wouldn't do her like that know what I mean, I wouldn't do her like that, know what I'm saying." DisVon was standing on the street corner.

"Von why is the body sitting In traffic? Where are you?"

"I'm standing on the corner...I can see her but mane I can't jump back in there know what I mean?" DisVon pointed at the ambulance as he talked, but he was done with this.

"Where is Wilson?" Lee-Lee asked.

"He had to see about Charles nem, and the police."

"The police!! They had a wreck?"

"Lee-Lee get somebody come get this lady.... I'm done, I can't do this! " DisVon hang up. His new career was over. Then DisVon saw his uncle across the street, always begging. Then he saw DisVon.

" Von! Von!" he crossed over carrying his brown bag underneath his arm. "Nephew let Unc git $20!" DisVon had an idea.

"OK drive this truck up to Dyes for me and I'll be right behind you." DisVon looked honest and sincere.

"I'll drive that clean %/<*^=#@#$!!" Ain't nobody in there is it? Unk was scratching his right hip with the free hand.

"Nawl Unk just a suit hanging up in the back that's all. Gone on I'll be behind you in my car." Unk got excited.

"BET NEPHEW!" Unk walked out in traffic turned the flashers off and made the next block. DisVon called Lee-Lee to let her know that the body was on its way. Wilson, Big John, Charles, SonnyBoy pulled up to the light and Charles spotted him. As he was pointing, the others saw him.

"DisVon where that body?" Wilson yelled out the window looking puzzled and nervous.

"She raised up man, that woman got up back there man! Ainnn gone be able man" They pulled the truck over.

" Man what you do with the body?"

"My Unk gone with her! I done messed up my clothes man!! Ainn gone be able bru!" Everyone in the truck laid over laughing, they laughed so hard until DisVon started to laugh as well.

" Von get in man, get in between Charles and SonnyBoy!"

"Naawl don't put his pissy tail in here by me! Told chall dat boy wasn't gone work out!! HIs head too lil!" SonnyBoy hitting his leg laughing...

"Boy we all had some of those moments!"

"Hell the dead can't do nothing to ya but make ya hurt chaself!"

'Shuuucks Mane I passed out on the street in the traffic mane! My legs gave out!" DisVon getting his frustration out.

"Then Unk came over here begging... so I told him take the wagon on back to Dyes and I'll be behind him! Mane ainnnn able bru...."

"Which Uncle?"
By the time they made the block Unc was running like he was about to pass the baton with his brown bag in his hand.

"Unk! Unk!" DisVon was yelling as loud as he could. Unk didn't even look back. The ambulance door was open and Willie was standing there about to remove the body.

"What happened Will?" Willie was so tickled he could barely stand up.

"I told him I came to help get the body out and he looked like he was gone pass out but he kicked in another gear and got down!"
By this time an old blue Low Rider pulled up... blowing the horn and all kinds of cussing was flying out of the windows..... and who but Doris came bolting through the funeral home doors waving and yelling,

"Nawl Clarence!! Gone on Clarence!!"
Nobody knew what was going on. Wilson was helping Charles get a body out, while Big John tried to help Willie get the body out. SonnyBoy begin to walk out towards Clarence to find out what was going on had no clue he was walking into the line of fire.

   "Sonny!!! Mr. Sonny!" Nori came running out the building trying to stop Mr. Sonny from getting hurt and tripped over a rock and down she went. Nori rolled like she was in combat train-ing...Wilson slung that body back in the truck and ran for it.
"NORI!" Wilson was in slow motion and Nori was rolling like she had oil and water on her suit.... it was too much!

CHAPTER 7

The Viewing in the Chapel

(dedicated to Catina Davidson-Brown)
Doris swung the door of that blue low rider open, "I didn't tell you to bring yo tail down here acting a fool. I just told you what SonnyBoy said! I don't want no trouble Clance! I work hea... gone back to the house now!"

"You my woman! SonnyBoy ain't got no business sayin nuttin to you nigh!" Clarence had his spicy peanuts and grape soda between his legs. "He got one mo time nigh Doris, One Mo and it ain't gone be no stopping me, I'm coming in like a Tsunami next time!" Clarence turned his peanuts up and drank the soda behind it. He had his shirt unbuttoned with his wife beater showing, his blue cap turned backwards on top of nappy permed hair, he was a cross between Snoop and Eazy E.

"Move woman!" he slammed his truck door and revved up the engine. He drove off playing Choosey Lover.

Meanwhile, Wilson and SonnyBoy had gotten Nori up and got her in the building. SonnyBoy still didn't know that Clarence had come for him.

"Nori you just stay in the office, we'll get ready for the Wake in 30 minutes for ya. I know you don't wanna see that old stuck up gal kno how! Me and the crew got this," SonnyBoy was in work mode. Wilson nodded at SonnyBoy,

"Thanks SonnyBoy I'll be in there to help y'all shortly, some more stuff came for the Wake it's in the back...a big picture, wreath and a sign-in book. Just tell Lee-Lee she can do that!"

"I got it mane ain new here" SonnyBoy walked out closing the door behind. The laughter was coming from the conference room, everyone laughing about the recap of the day.... they were all laughing as Big John was showing how every-thing went down on the street. SonnyBoy cut em off,

"Yall turkeys come on we got a show in about 30 minutes and this woman already messy... so let's make this thing run smoothly." Everyone started getting up and heading to the chapel to set up.
DisVon had come back looking very handsome, the youngest guy in the group looking like Puffy Combs, had his shades on and his cuff links. This was his first showing. Lee-Lee and Cymphonee were in place, Willie was ready, he was dressed looking like Grady from Sanford & Sons. Cym-phonee looked a little ghetto-gothic, she was cool with a whole different type of fan. Everything was in place, Mr. Kilgore Frank's lye their looking like money. He had on an all white suit, white bow tie, white gloves. White cane on top of him with a brown handle, white casket, with his name writ-

ten in cursive on the bottom, his make up was very natural, his hair was just as beautiful as if he was still a baby. He wore a slight smirk, he cheated cancer, Mr. Franks was finally at peace. 82 years of life, snuffed out by a heart attack. As he would say,

"I just reached my prime." He was a gentle man unlike his wife, Mrs. Marie and daughter, the bougie Felicia Franks, and Dyes Funeral Services had reached their peak with both of them.

"They hea," SonnyBoy had put down the sign in book and joined the rest of the crew that had spiffed themselves up. The door opened and there was a long pause.... it was Felicia and Mrs. Marie both dressed like the body in the casket, all white. They both came in with their noses turned up in the air. The chapel was a beautiful place, a cozy place with three chandeliers down the middle aisle, hanging like grapes on a vine. It had white walls, with hardwood floors to match the hard-wood pulpit and hardwood podium, the room had dark brown banquet chairs with good cushion, this was one beautiful place. Yet and still the hell bats were on the loose.

"Welcome to Dyes Fun," Lee-Lee tried to get out but was cut off,

'Why is the casket open?" Felicia began her foolishness.

"It'd be very hard to see through this casket, young lady!" SonnyBoy barged in. "If you want it down, we can close it back up!"

"Nonsense!" She walked closer and looked in on her daddy. "Papaw," she rubbed his glove that was fixed on his cane. Her mother came behind and placed her hands on the casket

"Kilgore is beautiful" she turned to Cymphonee, "I'm pleased," Cymphonee gave a little smile,

"Thank you Mrs. Franks!" Felicia's pawpaw whisper was getting louder and louder. By this time, Charles was slowly coming in, gout had him walking at an all time slow. Charles had put his dress up clothes on and his hair had waved up nicely. He smiled as he saw the crew standing to one side with their hands behind their backs. It was a proud moment.
Felicia began to scream out,

"Close it!!! Close the casket! I don't want nobody looking at my daddy! He's looking like a clown!" Felicia turned to run, and ran dead over Charles' feet with her red bottoms on. Charles let out a holler as if he was a teen wolf. That pressure from Felicia's wide feet took him down, as he was headed down the only thing he could grab, Have Mercy, was Mrs. Marie's skirt to catch his fall. He was going down in slow motion for the second time today. He grabbed Mrs. Marie's skirt, which was no support at all, everyone was reaching to no avail, it happened! The skirt came down- as well as Mrs. Marie, the pink silk bloomers popped out like a Jack in the box. Charles broke her fall, because she landed on top of him, but her legs went up and kicked the casket. The casket shook violently, everyone then tried to catch the casket that almost tilted over on the both of them.

"Lord Jesus! Lord JESUS!" Mrs. Marie skirt was caught up around her knees and she was scuffling trying to pull them up. After SonnyBoy and DisVon secured the casket they tried to pull Mrs. Marie off Charles to not cause any more harm to his poor tender feet. But Mrs. Marie was swinging her arms, she didn't want to stand up with her bloomers showing. Cymphonee and Lee-Lee were trying to help, but Lee-Lee's little body gave over to a laughing spirit, she was trying to hold it in until tears were falling from her face. She fought the laugh until her body just came to a shake... it was uncontrollable. When Cymphonee noticed the shaking, she realized what was happening she tried not to look, just to keep from laughing... now they both were weak.... they didn't have the strength to pull Mrs. Marie's skirt over her hips.

"Yall some weak little chirens," Marie had broke into a sweat and chewing her gum even faster. As those words rolled off her tongue.... all her help had failed. Lee-Lee's attempts to hold it in came out like a dam had busted... tears fell from her face and the home laugh escaped....followed by Cymphonee's that ended up on the floor next to Charles and half dressed Mrs. Marie. DisVon walked off trembling all over. SonnyBoy couldn't hold his peace,

"Ainnnn never seen nothing like this!" His laughter filled the room and Mrs. Marie sounded like a hen laying an egg. Charles even had to laugh.

"What in the world going on here?" And then...... the devil dressed in white busted back in with fire in her eyes, but her dress was tucked in her pantyhose from the back to all the way around the side... she switched down the aisle but by the time she got to the front every soul in the chapel was slain in laughter. Nobody could tell her that her dress was stuck in her panty-hose.....Wilson come in to see what was going on and he was unable to help this time. He caught the back chair he couldn't go any further. The laughing gas was loose. Willie tried to tell Felicia her dress was tucked away in her pantyhose but she was busy trying to pull her mom up as her mom resisted and laughed uncontrollably. So Willie walks up and puts his hands on Felicia's back, she violently turns and pushes Willie into the casket....it was unbelievable at this moment, Willie and the casket rocked first and then slid across the floor... there was no one to help at this moment....DYES FUNERAL SERVICE was having a moment in time....

CHAPTER 8

A New Beginning

Nori sat on her orange chaise shaped in a U, and her tears flowed down her face. She didn't try to wipe them... she just needed them to escape her body. She learned a long time ago, some tears are meant to escape to help relieve pressure that's building. As they escaped She could feel weight lifting. (Have you ever had to just cry, letting tears escape your body in order for the pressure to go down? Think about how powerful those few drops of water are...I dare you to cry sometimes and let God catch your tears. Nothing is wrong with crying, I had to cry yesterday as I poured my heart out to God about my son that had been diagnosed with Covid and he was so far away. I couldn't get to him and he couldn't get to me, but when I told God all about it!! Now I feel like a Champion AGAIN)

ANYWAY NORI lye on that chaise with her hands in a praying position under her face as a pillow and the tears rolled down her hands and onto the chaise, a steady stream as her stomach was in a shifting gear motion. She was tired, she

was worn and she was weary. She had no one but Dyes Funeral Services as family. She felt so alone, she couldn't talk to them. Her mind thought about everyone she no longer had, her dad walked away when she was eleven, her mom had passed a few years earlier, no sisters, no brothers, no uncles or aunts that she knew of...."how could a person be so alone in the world?" (How could a person be so alone in a marriage? How could a person be so alone in a big family? On a job? In any type of relationship? Where does this alone time come from?)
She soon discovered as she heard a soft still voice,
      "I will never leave you. I will never walk away. I will be with you until the end of the earth." Goosebumps covered her arms, hair stood up on her neck. She knew who it was. She felt a fresh breeze in the room and there was no opened door, there was no window up. Then she felt a touch like no other, it swaddled her like a baby. She could only lye there in the arms of God. Peace came over her and worry and heartache slid under the door trying to find a way out of the house. There was no more room for anything that wasn't of God. She cried until she begin to cough, that made her purge... she ran to the bathroom and she begin to spit in her toilet, she felt differently. She felt like her life had been RESTARTED. She had been set free, she knew that she wasn't a bird but she felt like she could fly, she wasn't a cotton ball, but she felt so light, she wasn't running a fever but a warmness sat in her heart. She felt like she was being led to go somewhere but didn't know where, she felt like she had a lot to say, but didn't know what she was going to say.

She was feeling like she had never felt. She washed her face and put on some nice clothes, got into Rov and drove straight to the grocery store. She knew that her fridge was full, but she was needed at the grocery store. She got out walking fast looking around, unsure of what she was looking for but her gut told her to keep going. As she got inside, she wasn't led to grab a buggy, so she kept walking and heard the word, "8" she walked to aisle 8, and there was only a man there looking at mayonnaise. She became confused. And begin to doubt her gut. He looked up and saw her, "Hey daughter" the gentleman smiled showing all whites and a side gold. Nice looking older man, she perceived him to be a Man of God.
"Hey there!" She spoke back and begin to turn away in disappointment.
"You are in the right place at the right time, Nori." She stopped dead in her tracks. That was the same voice from earlier and he said her name. Before she could turn around...
(FOR YOU READING THIS it's time for you to give your alone time to GOD)

CHAPTER 9

Life is Filled with Surprises

She felt that fresh breeze again. As she turned to the gentleman that was looking very serious.

"You said my name" she walked back toward him. "How did you know my name?" Nori's heart was racing. He laughed.

"Well you do have a few billboards up my sister."

She grabbed her chest in relief. She just knew he would say God told him. But instead he says,

"God has given you a new beginning! Give God more of you. Everything else can wait. God knows the desires of your heart. He knows what you think about all the time, He knows that you hate being alone, that you want to go to another level in HIM. AND NOW IS THE TIME. The Lord said he sent some people in your life and they are not saved. These people have been assigned to you. If you watch their actions you won't see them, but if you listen to their heart and hear in the SPIRIT, you'll know. Don't let good works fool you, listen to the heart, it speaks." Nori was somewhat caught like a deer in the headlights. Tears rolled down her face,

"Pastor why would God want me to do this? I'm just a broken woman."

"Glad you asked daughter, when I was a little boy we had horses and I loved to ride." He placed his hands on the buggy and leaned over to Nori..."but each one we rode had to be broken in. You can't do nothing with a wild horse. But once you break em, they submit to your way, heeey! Hoooold! Go! Stop! They no longer have their own mind, but they submit to their Master's Will. Well alright my daughter, wife waiting on this mayonnaise."
He left so fast with the buggy it was like he was never there.

"Nori, Nori!" She felt like it was all a dream until she felt a tug not in her spirit but on her arm. Doris was pulling her arm.

"Nori. Is you alright honey? You just standing here staring at that mayonnaise like you was in cranse (transe) or something!"

"Oh no mam I was just talking to this gentleman and he knew my name and said some things that..."

"Mrs. Doris do you go to church?"

"Yes guh the good Lawd done been good to me and Clarence baby. Brought us through this and that. You know? What made you ask that?

"Just wondering, I'll talk to you later this evening at the wake Love. I have a few more errands to run. "
As she gets into the car, her phone rings.... the smile crept across her face as she answered,

"Sunshine!"

You already know who it was....
    "What you doing Boss Lady?"
She heard this voice at the right time....
    "Leaving the grocery store, what you doing?"
His smile was just as big.
    "I'm sitting out on my deck, stop by if you
have a minute."
She had only been alone with Wilson about 3
times unintentionally, she never wanted to be
alone with him, because of her underlying condi-
tions...her heart. It was so vulnerable at this
point. And Wilson was a hard worker, handsome,
very witty, he smelled nice, he dressed nice and
his heart seemed pure.
    "Nori! Can you stop by?"
    "Oh yes, I'm just over on Lincoln, pull up in
just a second!" She hang up and took a deep
sigh......
    "Lord you guide all of me.... this new begin-
ning need to line up with YOUR WILL LORD." As
she whipped the Rover in the driveway....Wilson
was standing there in his black basketball shorts
a white tee, gold teeth shinning, chain shinning,
and he had on some furry pink house shoes with
his toes sticking out.
Nori wondered what was up with that... she was
met at the door with a hug and a forehead kiss.
Nothing to dramatic it was friendly fire LOL.
    "Come on Sunshine!" She got out with the
biggest smile. She was led by Wilson to the side of
his home where she could hear some oldies music
playing, she could hear women laughing before
she could bend the corner.... so now what was she
about to experience, an unintentional heartbreak.
She took a deep breath and there they were 3
beautiful women, one in a house coat, and 2 in

pajamas. Nori's heart stopped. She knew Wilson was fine and had it going on, but not like this. She almost lost her sight. She didn't want to see. They all jumped up and greeted her, except the one with the pink robe that belonged to the shoes that Wilson was wearing.

"You're Sunshine!! They both grabbed her hands and kissed her cheek and then hugged her like they knew her. Nori was really at a loss and Wilson was all smiles.

"Sunshine these are my two sisters, Keshia and Jaki." She was so relieved. Wilson grabbed Nori's hand and led her to the pink robed one,
"This is Mama!" And he gave Nori's hands to his mom. She took her hands and trapped them inside hers.
"You are blessed in the city, blessed in the fields blessed when you come and go!" God has given somethings into your hands that are precious to Him, He trust you with those that He's given you. What you do they will follow. What you say they will listen." She took Nori's hands and gave them back to Wilson. As she pushed Wilson closer to Nori. She began to laugh....
"Boss Lady huh?" You are as beautiful as Wilson has been describing to us on the phone." The mother eyes glowed as she looked at Wilson as he gazed at Nori.
"Now baby... this is your husband after he gets saved." Nori was really in shock about all that was taking place. It seemed like everything was hap-pening so fast.
"First it is so nice to finally meet you all. I have heard so much about you. I didn't know you

guys were this beautiful. I thought you guys were Wilson's women are something." They all laughed." And his wife?" Nori laughed but she was the only one laughing.

CHAPTER 10

Heart Block

Nori's laugh was cut short, after she noticed that everyone was looking serious. She thought to herself.

"Are they pranking me?"

"This isn't a joke Sunshine, you're all I think about. The thought of you being alone hurts my heart because I know you're my wife but when the time is right. It's not a coincidence I'm always trying to help, that I drive by your house at night to make sure you're ok. I know that I'm the man for you, but when the time is right. There isn't another woman or anything it's just loose ends that have got to be tied up. And as soon as they are tied I'm coming for my Sunshine." Wilson caressed Nori's face and kissed her tears. Your tears from now on will be of laughter and joy."

"Tell her son, that's my gentleman I raised." The sister's joined in and they all hugged Wilson and Nori.

"Come eat with us!" Wilson rubbed his hands together. We got your favorite cheese grits with shrimp, baby sis made Mimosas, French toast, ham and hashbrowns, pineapples, kiwis, jalapeños and strawberries, it all sounded so good to Nori but she could not comprehend all that was said to her.

"Awww yes well I need to be going get some things together we got a Wake in the chapel today at..."

"At 4 Sunshine, it's handled."

"Yes well I really need to speak to you alone. I'm not really sure of what's going on or what just happened here."
He realized that Nori was uncomfortable. He took her hand and led her back to her truck.

"I'm sorry I know this caught you off guard. But I really love you and I think that you feel the same way about me. I just wanted you to know that neither of us are on the market anymore. I want to be in your life and I think you want to be in mine."
Wilson waited, the pause he was hoping that she would jump in and say yes it was only silence and even though she wanted to say yes her mouth wouldn't cooperate.

"Am I wrong?" This handsome young man stood there with his heart in his hands ready to give it to his Sunshine. He had a smiled that was brighter than the sun foreal. As Nori looked into his eyes, blinded by the gold, she was mute. His smile began to fade, he knew for sure they felt the same thing. But what was it? He didn't even have words right here. A lump came in his throat and he felt his tears about to release. He opened Nori's door, she turned to get in and before she could close it. He closed the door and walked away before a tear could fall. She crank the truck with her heart in her lap. She could not under-

stand what just happened. This is what she wanted, her heart wanted this, her lips wanted this, her mind was set on this and here was the moment and her mouth could not say what her heart felt. She drove away with tears flowing again today. They were not tears of joy. What was happening. Wilson's heart was so heavy he used the front door, he didn't want his family to know that his Sunshine had turned to midnight. What a surprise this was. How could this be?
Nori's heart was so overwhelmed that she pulled over at a store. She sobbed. What was happening to her. Why couldn't she grab her happiness?
[Answer this: What would you do in this situation? Why couldn't she talk? What about Wilson?
Man my heart is so full right now.
Sometimes God put our answered prayers in front of us but He won't make us pick them up. If you never try a thing.... you'll never know. We've learned to forgive others but we won't forgive ourselves, we think we don't deserve happiness, peace and love. Forgive yourself so that you can have an abundance
Let me know what you guys think!

CHAPTER 11

When the Bottom Falls Out

Nori's flood gate had opened up. She just couldn't wrap her mind around what happened. She looked in the mirror, she was a mess. This morning had been a roller coaster. And to top it all off, SonnyBoy pulls up next to her. He gets out and walks to her window. Nori let her window down.

"Hey gal you alright? I saw you when you pulled in, looked like you were fighting with yourself." SonnyBoy loved Nori like a daughter and realized that she was dealt a sour hand. Even though he tries not to show he loves her, he really does.

"If you don't wanna talk, I understand, hell I don't like fa people to be in my business either. But I will tell you this. That young man down the street, he loves you. I don't know if he's the reason you fighting, but I saw your truck over there. Ain't none of my business but I think his heart fa you. He's genuinely honest to be a young man at his age. All he know, Sunshine this, Sunshine that, Boss lady this and......I said boy you already hen pecked and I betcha ain't kista yet." SonnyBoy laughed. Nori smirked....

"IT"S JUST HARD TO TRUST MR. SONNY...."

"BABY," SonnyBoy cut her off.... ever since Doris left me 20 something years ago for Clarence Jones!!!! Whewwww talk about hurt....Doris was a goodt woman. She a lil crazy in the head some-times.... but I never thought she would leave me, I took her for granted and this cock-eyed, banana boat, long mouf" SonnyBoy gritted his teeth like he could just taste him.

" Mr. Sonny just let it go!" We win some and lose some."
He propped against the truck,
 "Nori, 'Tell me gal, did you lose today? Cause you looking rough out in here in this parking lot.... you are a woman of caliber.... go fix it. Doris had waited on me for 3 days to fix it.... on that 4th day she got up like Lazarus.... she came out that house and ooo Clarence consoled her. He knew how much I love-did Doris. He swept her up like an eagle picking up his prey. Ain't nothing you just got scared that's all. You will never know if he'll hurt you, if you don't give him the chance not to. Go handle your business fo ppl see you outchea like this."
Nori had no words, she started the truck and pulled back up to Wilson's house but his Hellcat was gone. She called and no answer, now what? She drove around and it looked like every street she saw SonnyBoy lol or was it her mind.

"Lord if this is real, if this is the man for me, that YOU want me to have. Fix it! I'm tired of crying today." chills came over her body as she

was slowing down to stop at the funeral
home..."Go home"
She looked behind to see what she was hearing...

"Go home" out of curiosity she kept driving
headed home. "I'm not going to try to call him
again. He'll see my missed calls. How could he
put me in this predicament."
As she pulled up there was the Hellcat in the
driveway. Her heart sank. She pulled up next to it.
And out comes Wilson. He looked as if he had
been crying and she looked as if she had been
fighting.
He opened her door and Nori fell into his arms.
They both had so much to say.... until they were
running over each other with their words.

"I love you Wilson!" Nori didn't stutter her
words didn't get locked up....

"I know you do Sunshine that's why I'm here. I
know you were overwhelmed and it hurted to
think that you didn't but my heart doesn't lie, I
know how you feel. That's how I know you're my
wife. I had been praying for a wife trying to figure
out where I needed to be. I was in the wrong
place with the wrong person. I'm in the process of
getting a divorce. That's why I moved here, to
start over. I filed for my divorce the day I moved
away. It won't be long, it's been a year since I
spoke with my ex wife, she's waiting as well. I
don't have any children and I don't have any soul
ties with any woman. I'm just a man in love with
his boss lady. Nori Dyes will you be my lady?"

"Yes!" Nori smiled with confidence. Their eyes
locked and their lips met. Wilson tears met Nori's
and you can just hear the windchimes chiming all
around as the wind picked up.

A moment stamped in time. A horn blew it was SonnyBoy F250... he kept on rolling.

"The WAKE"

Everyone was getting to the wake an hour before time to make sure everything runs smoothly. SonnyBoy was feeling so good he stopped and got everyone food.

"Cymphonee I'm so glad that SonnyBoy didn't know that Clarence had
pulled up here to get him girl!" Cymphonee and Lee-Lee laughed.

"Come git who!" SonnyBoy busted in and threw the burgers on the table and some rolled off on the other side. He was hotter than a hornet caught up in a ruffle dress.

" Clarence come at me?" Lee-Lee and Cymphonee were at a loss for words.

"No Mr. Sonny we weren't talking about you. Something happened last night at Cymphonee house." SonnyBoy temper was jumping on the side of his head,

'OK enlighten me cause I'm curious " SonnyBoy wasn't buying the lie. Lee-Lee was so glad when she heard Big John and DisVon come in. Cymphonee jumped up,

"Whew let me make sure my gal ready back here!"

"Nawl ain't nobody leaving til someone tell me about Clarence coming up here to git me!" SonnyBoy had leaned over on the table with his knuckles propping him up. His dress pants were hung up on the top of his boots.

'Hey everyone!" Doris came in with a great attitude and Clarence was close behind her. What a day to bring your man to work!!

"Hey SonnyBoy, Doris came in with 2 gallons of sweet tea and Clarence close behind with a tray of tacos.
Lee-Lee looked at Cymphonee and Cymphonee looked at the floor.
"How's it going ladies" Clarence was a gentlemen but when he looked at SonnyBoy and SonnyBoy heard his voice their eyes met up like a Western Show down....Clarence slung the tray of tacos on the table and he got in a stance like karate kid.....
"Oooooo no Clarence not today! The devil is a liar!!" She got in between the two with her arms stretched apart.
"You a slu foot dog Clarence!" SonnyBoy yelled over Doris's arm as if it was a fence.
" Well Doris like it!" Clarence smiled.
That hit SonnyBoy in the throat that hurt, he loved Doris. SonnyBoy ran around the other side of the table and slid down on one of the burgers that came out of the bag and hit his head on the floor. Everyone ran around the table trying to get SonnyBoy up.But no one could wake him.